Disney · PIXAR

WALL·E

LOTS OF BOTS

By Kiki Thorpe
Illustrated by Ben Butcher

Disney PRESS
New York
An Imprint of Disney Book Group

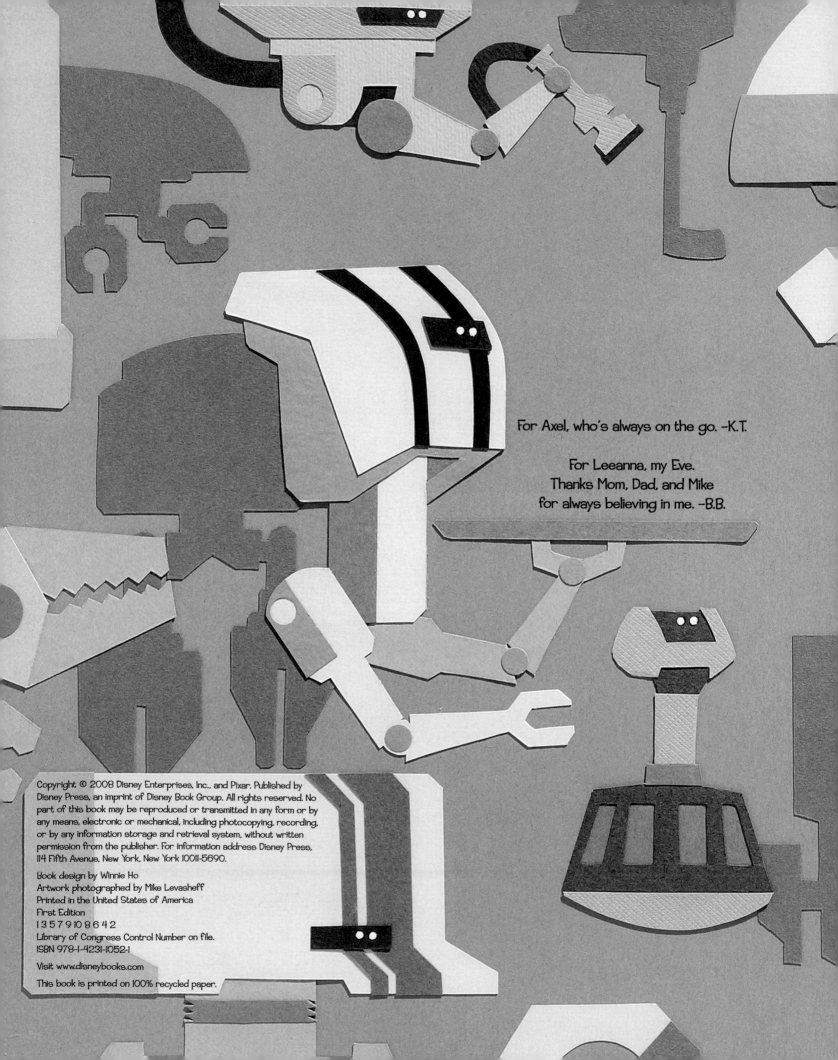

For Axel, who's always on the go. —K.T.

For Leeanna, my Eve.
Thanks Mom, Dad, and Mike
for always believing in me. —B.B.

Book design by Winnie Ho
Artwork photographed by Mike Levasheff
Printed in the United States of America
First Edition
1 3 5 7 9 10 8 6 4 2
Library of Congress Control Number on file.
ISBN 978-1-4231-1052-1

Visit www.disneybooks.com

This book is printed on 100% recycled paper.

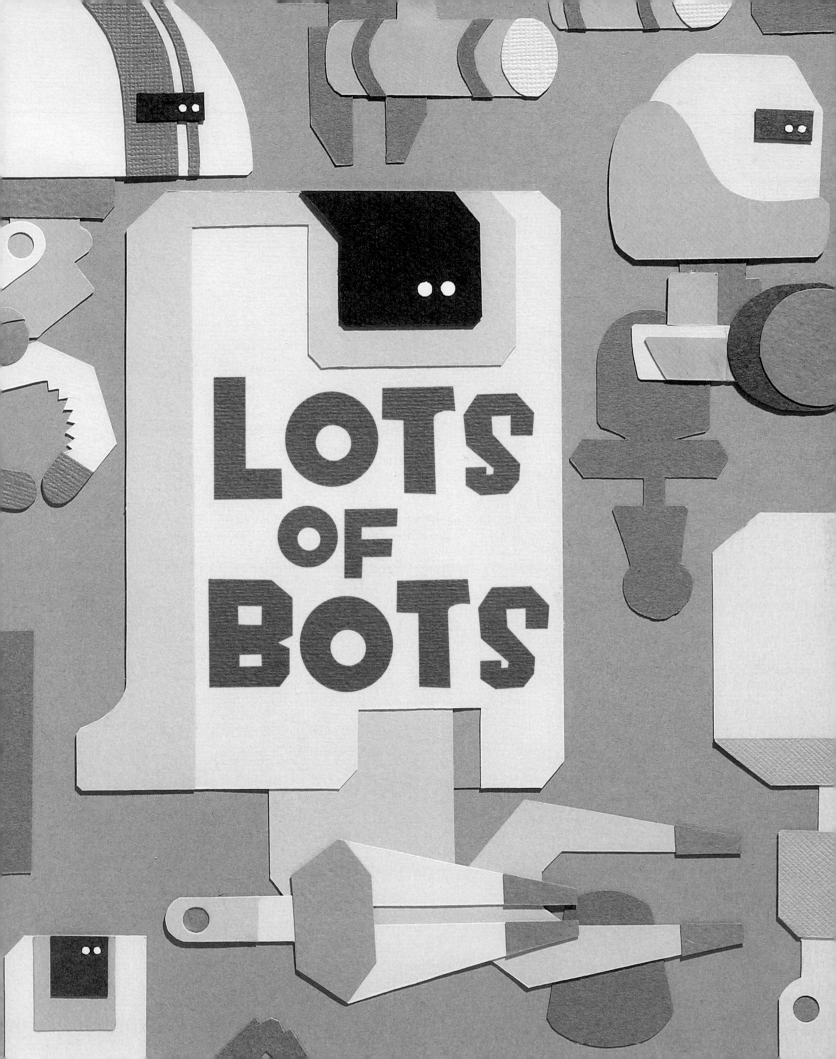

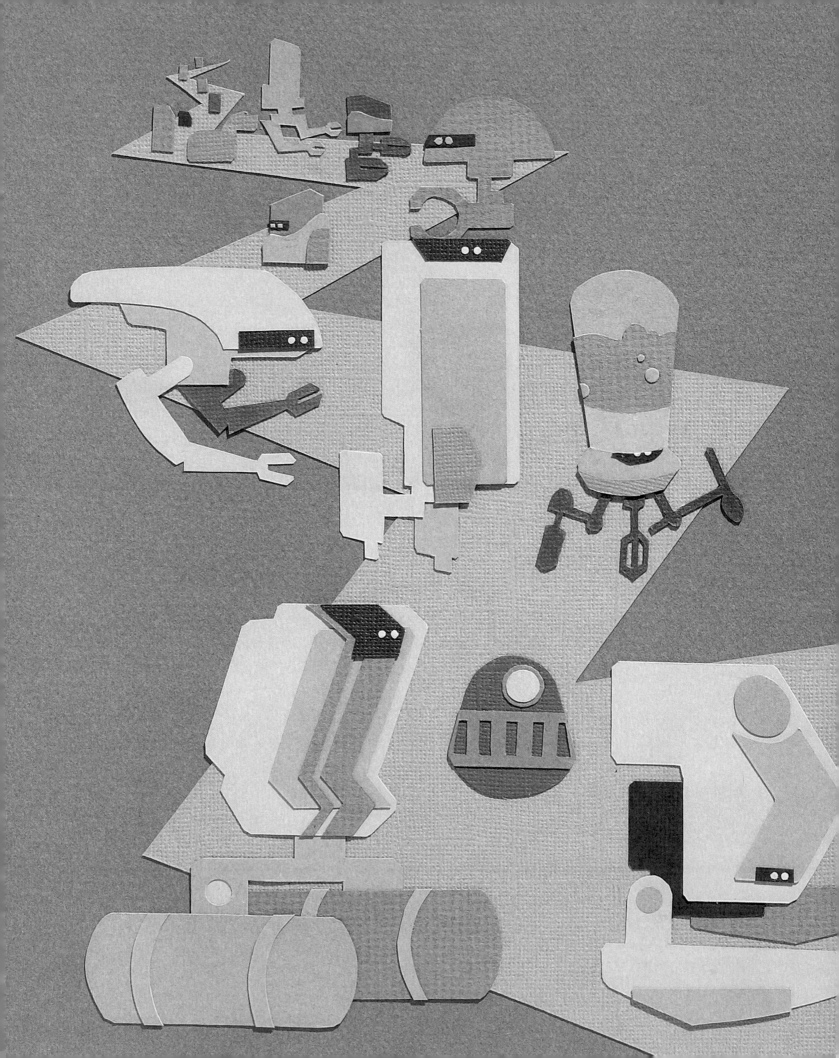

Robots.
Robots.

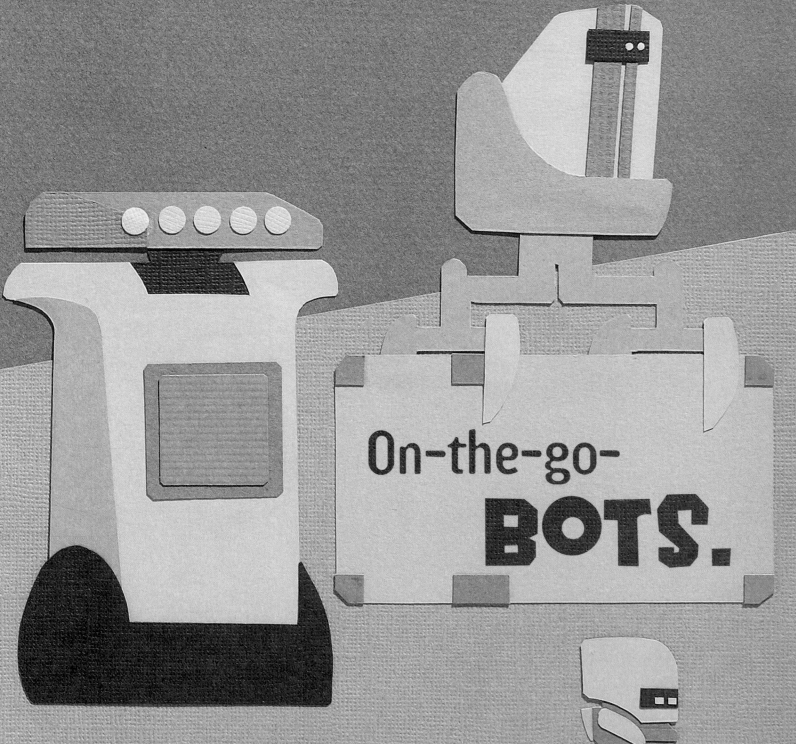

On-the-go-
BOTS.

BIG-
machine-bots.

Rolling.

FLASHING.

Beeping.

DASHING.

Scooting.

Sneaking.

HIDING.

Peeking.

Searching ship from end to end,
looking for his special friend.

Line up, robots!

One, two, three.

Do the work efficiently.

Look Out!

Robots coming through.

Each one has a job to do.

Scrub-bot **SCOURS.**

Spray-bot **SHOWERS.**

Paint-bot **coats.**

Crane-bot **totes.**

Tractor-bot **TUGS.**

Forklift-bot LUGS.

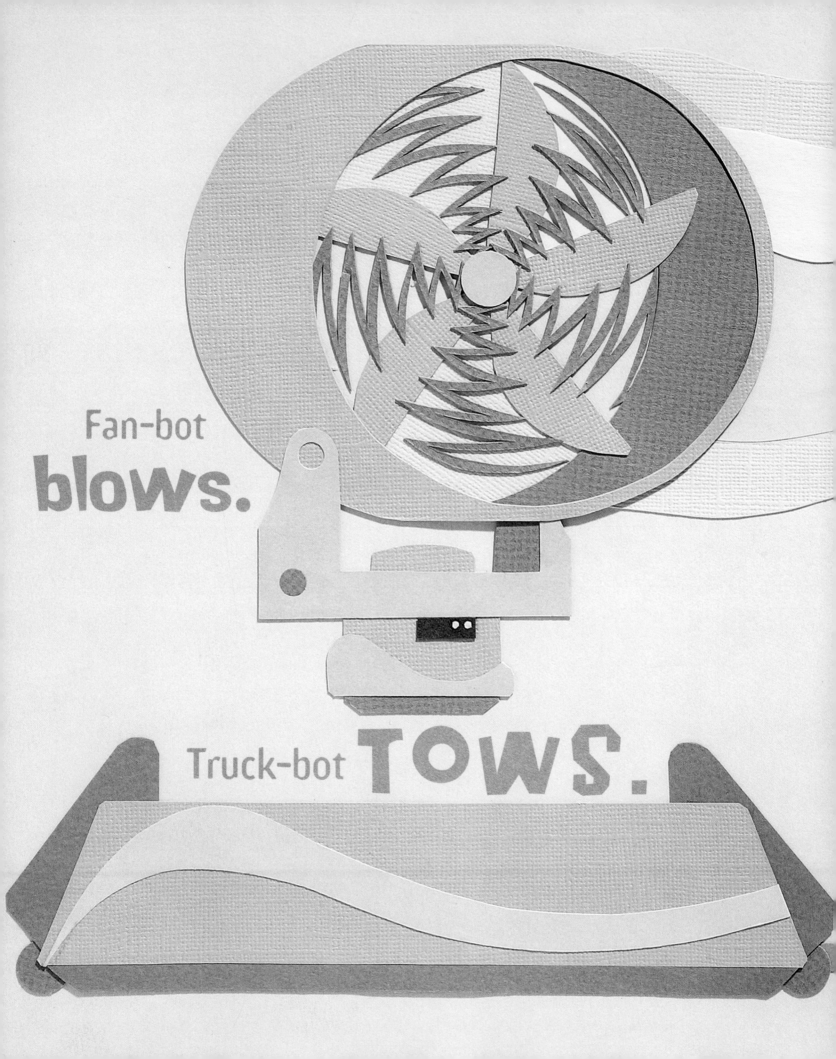

Fan-bot **blows.**

Truck-bot **TOWS.**

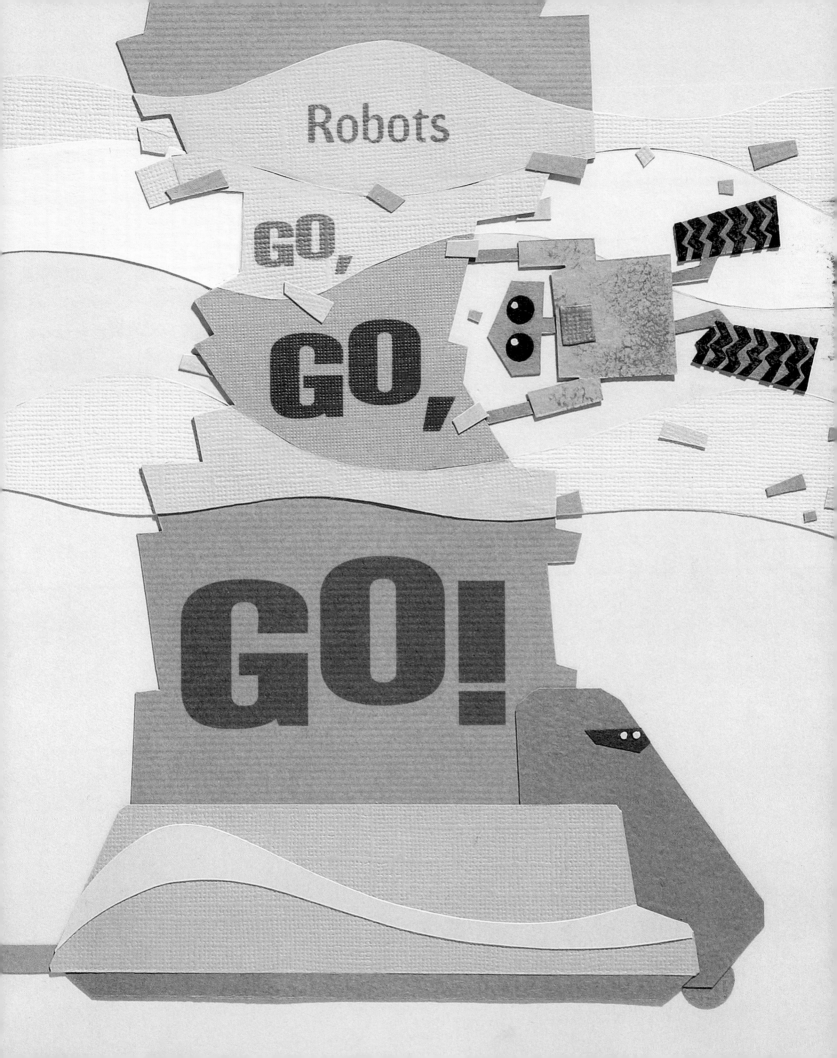

WALL•E sees a bot for every chore. But where's the one he's looking for?

There she is!
At last he sees her.
He can't wait.
He has to reach her.

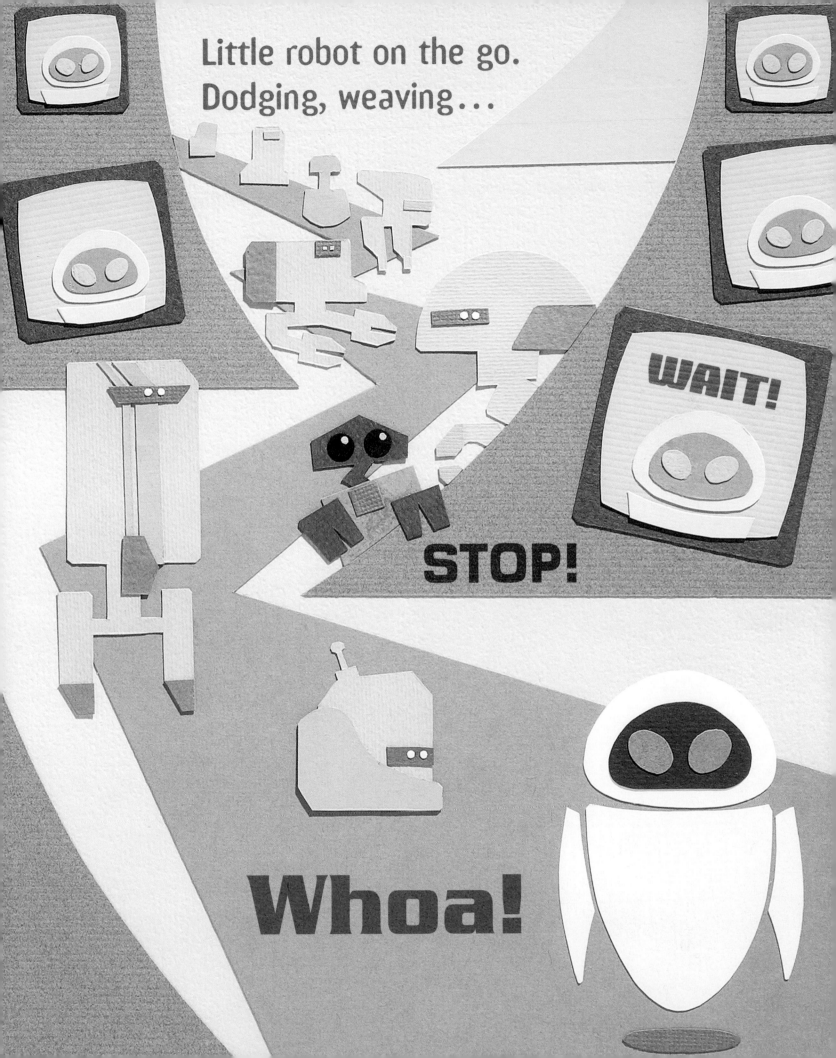

Tractor-bot **crashes.**

Forklift-bot **smashes.**

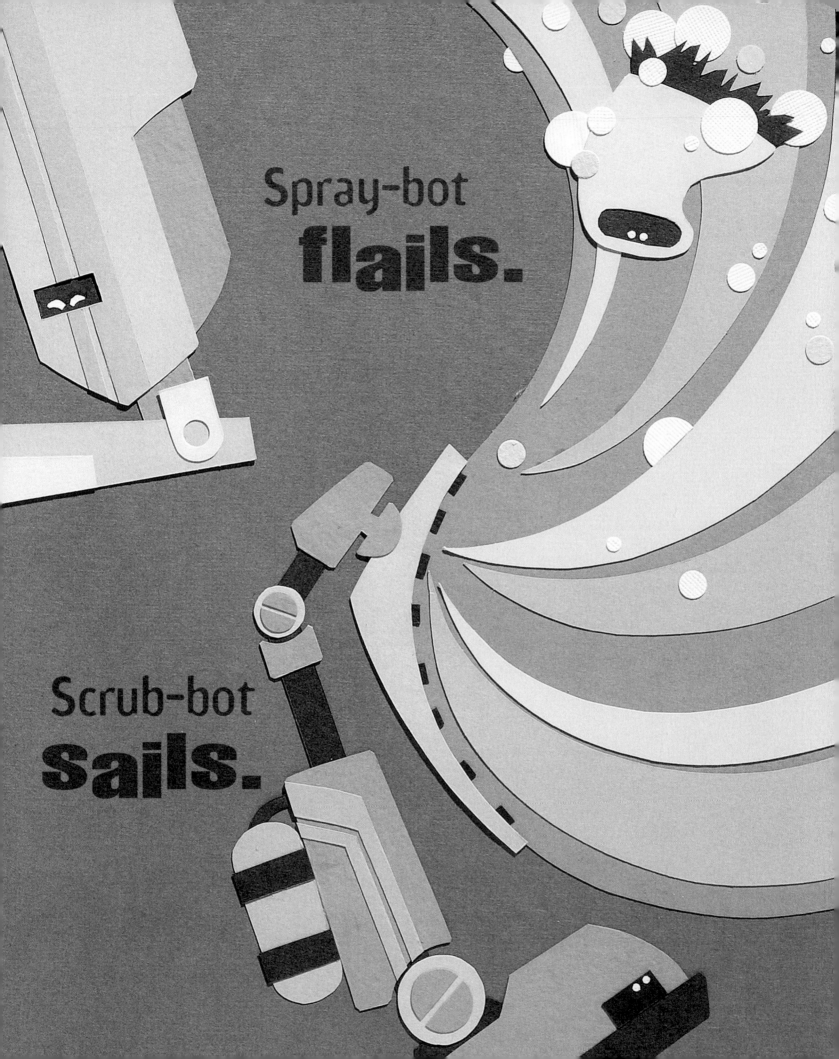

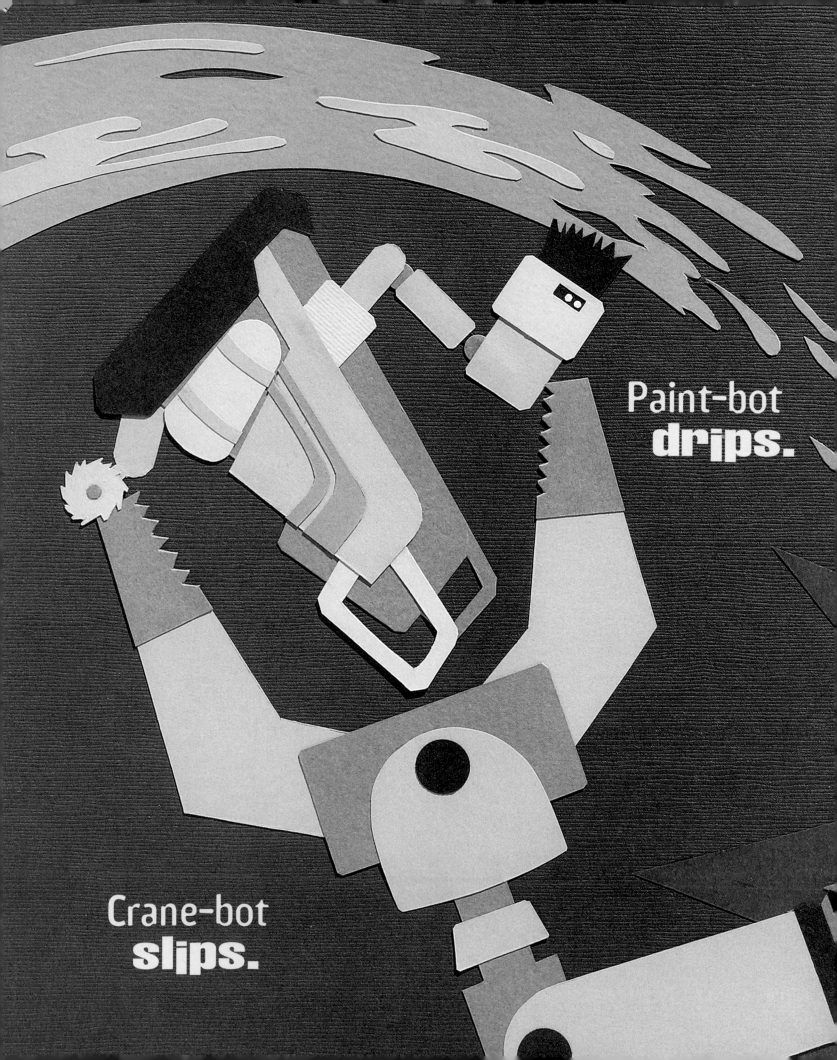

Fan-bot **throws.**

Amp-bot **blows.**

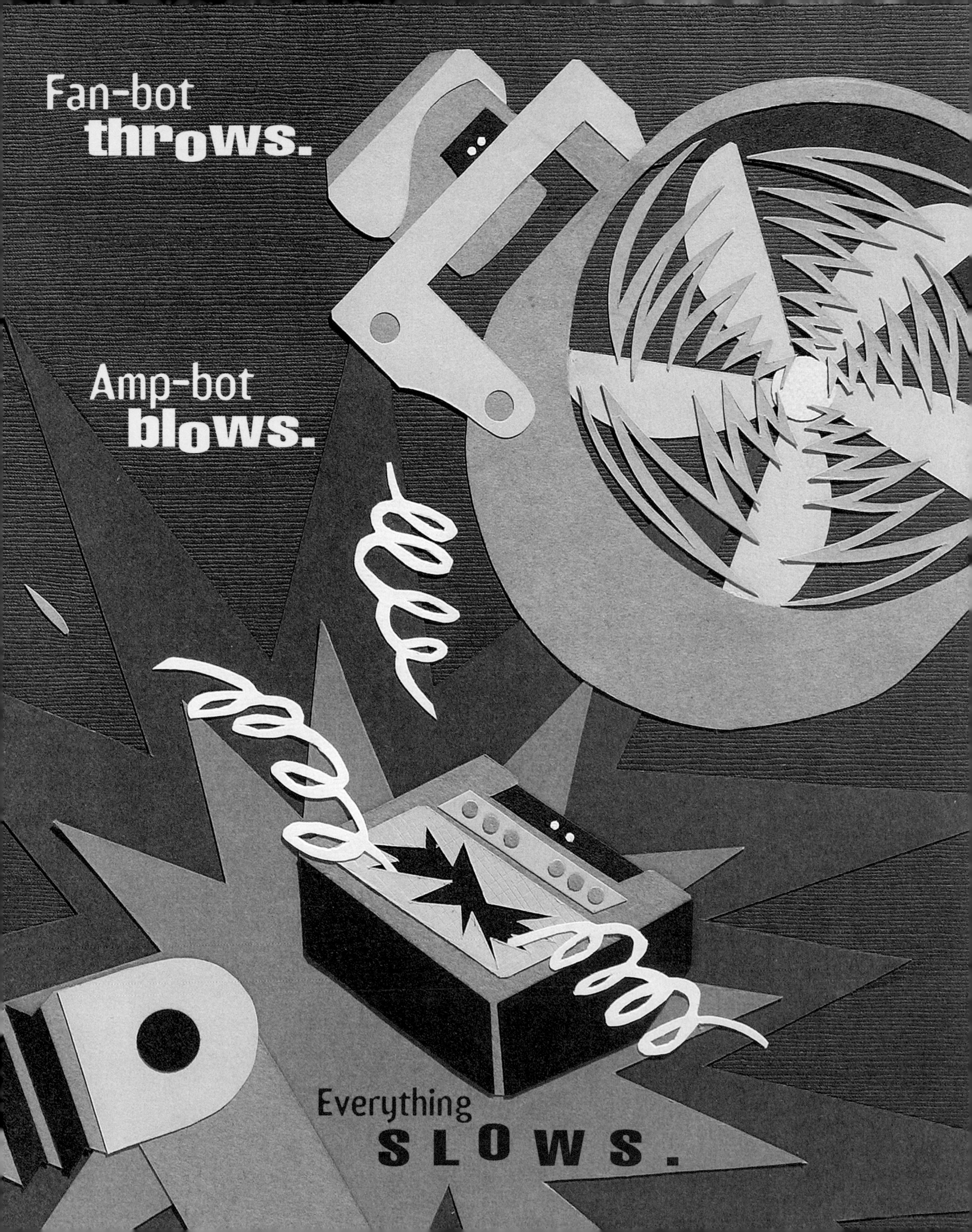

Everything **SLOWS.**

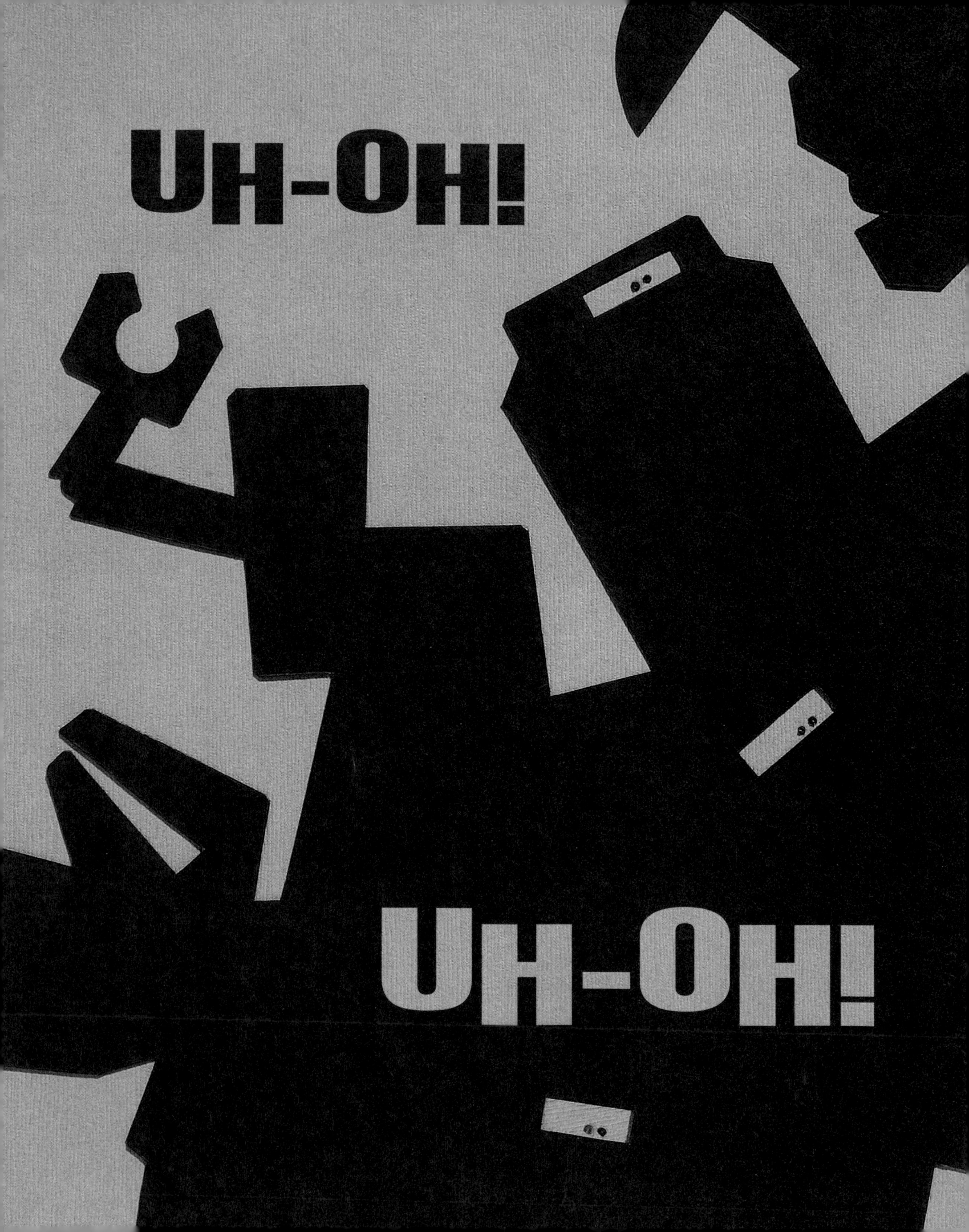
UH-OH!
UH-OH!

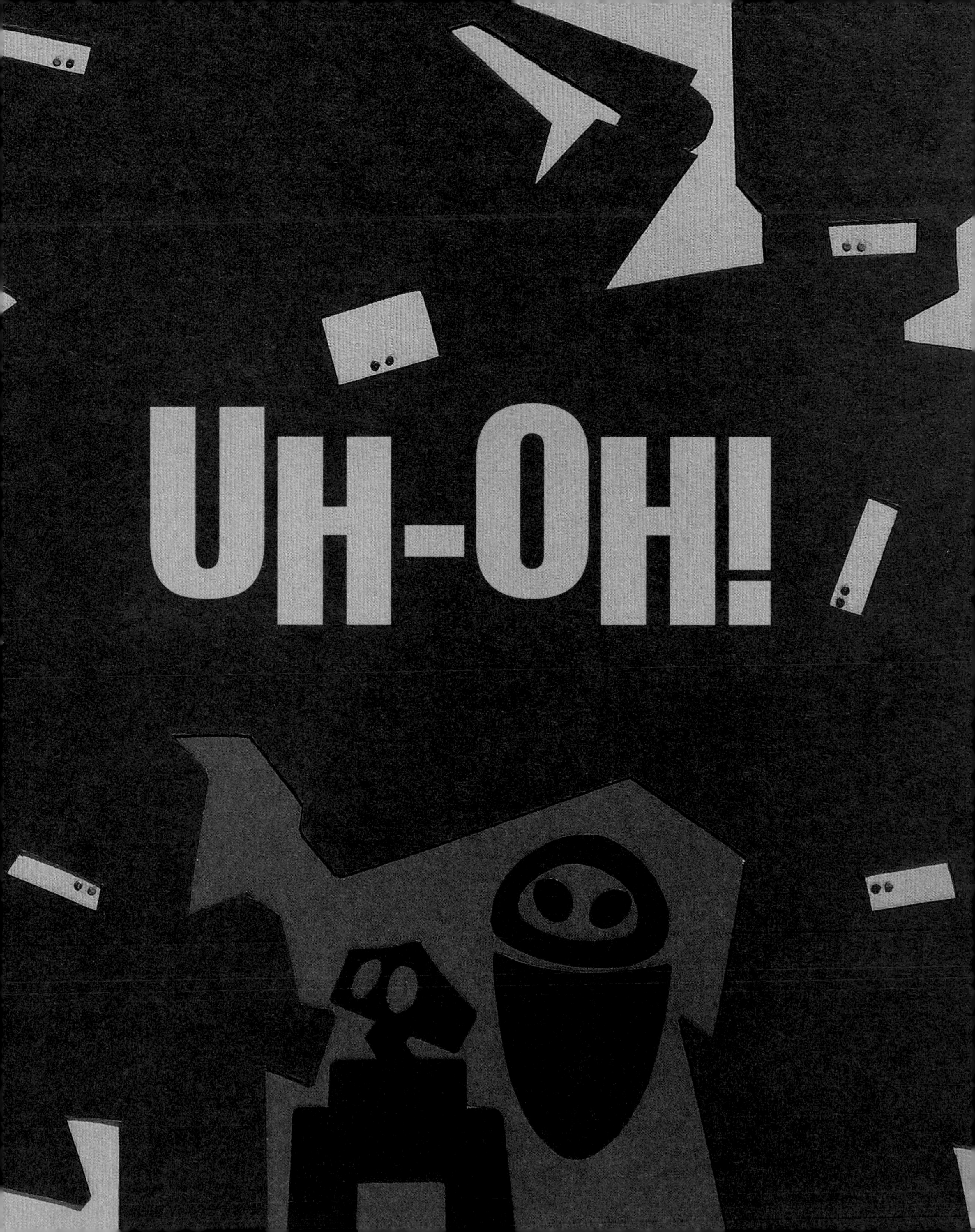

UH-OH!

Alarms are
blaring.

Robots are
staring.

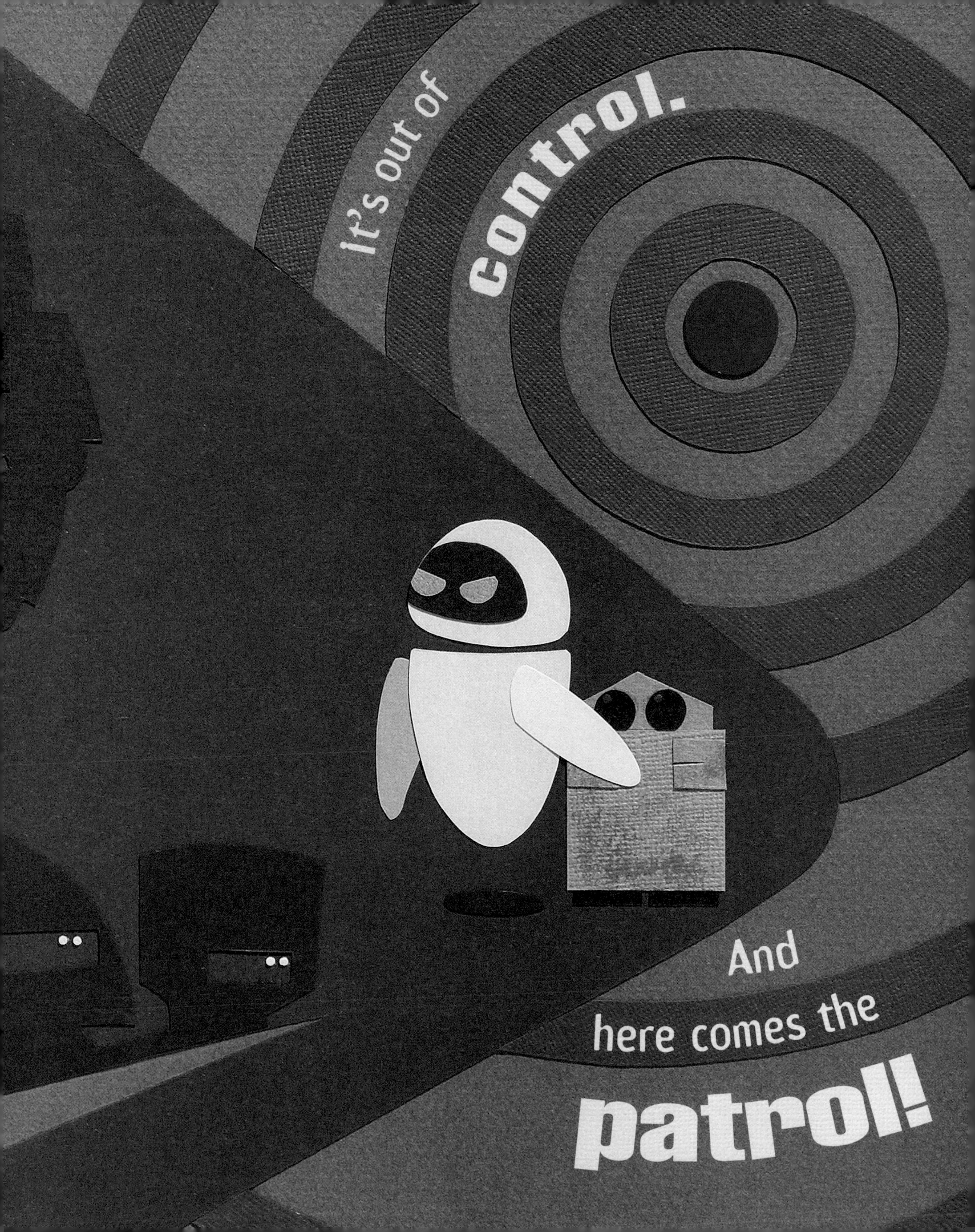
It's out of
control.
And
here comes the
patrol!

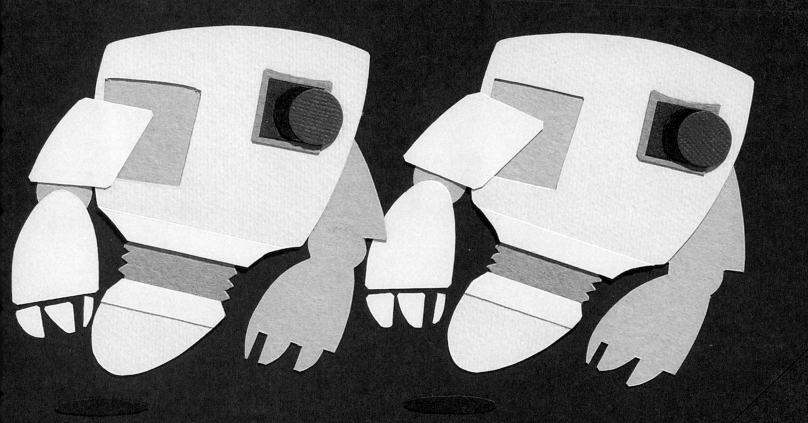

Run **BOTS!**
Race **BOTS!**
Being-chased- **BOTS.**

Can't get through!
Only one thing to do.

Music **playing.**

Robots **swaying.**

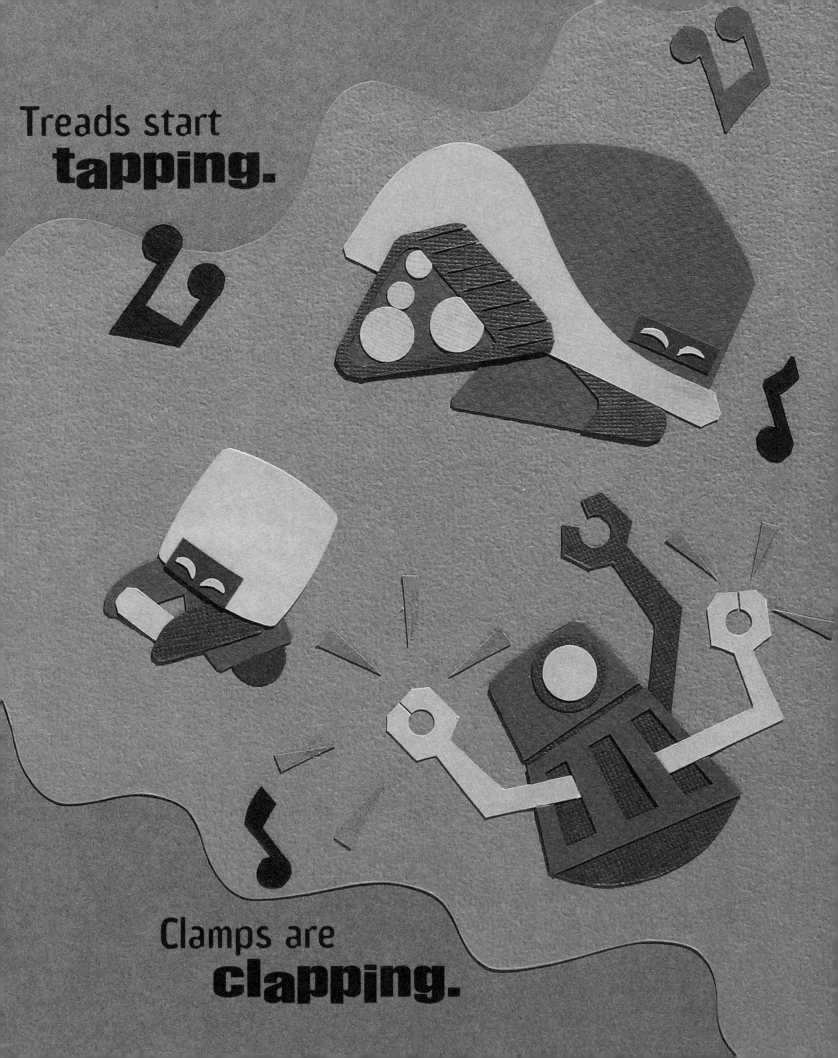

Tractor-bot
jumping.

Forklift-bot
pumping.

Crane-bot **swinging.** Paint-bot **slinging.**

Robots . . . **SINGING!**

Robots dancing,
   having fun.

Patrol-bots now are
on the run.

Little-clever-
BOTS!

Now-or-never-
BOT . . .

Friends-forever BOTS.

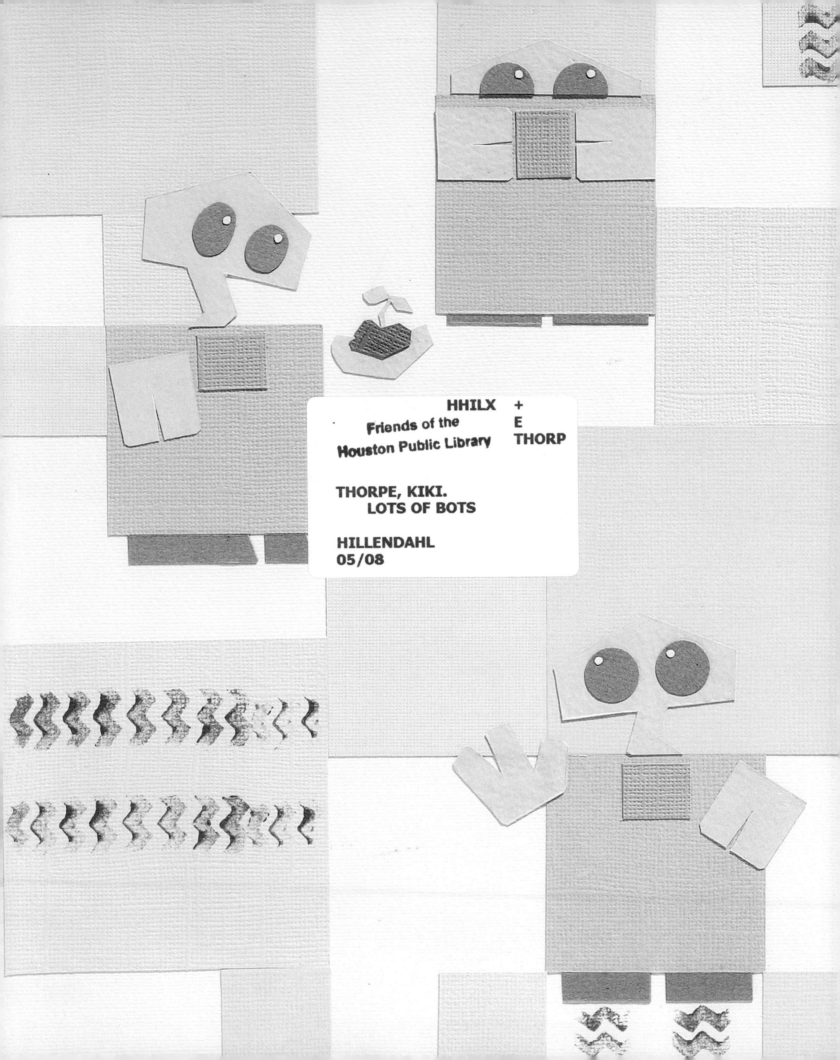